AF425614

ISBN : 979-8-9850950-1-2
Library of Congress Control Number: 2022903190

www.writtencreatively.com

For my little ninja,
may you always find joy
in playing pretend.

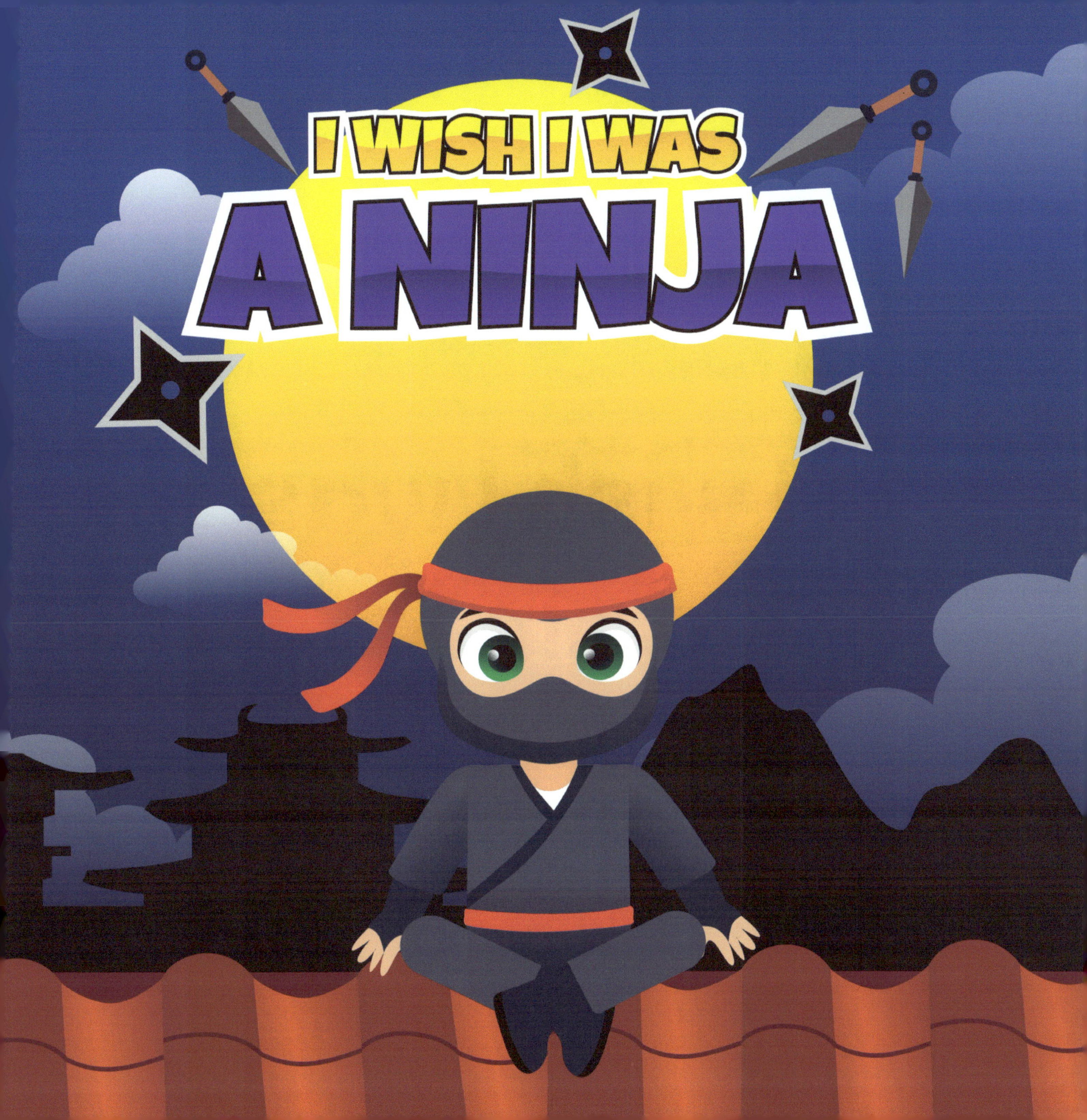

I WISH I WAS
A NINJA

I wish I was
a ninja.

What do you think of that?

Slipping through the shadows,

As quiet as
a cat.

I wish I was
a ninja.

I'd jump, and climb, and run.

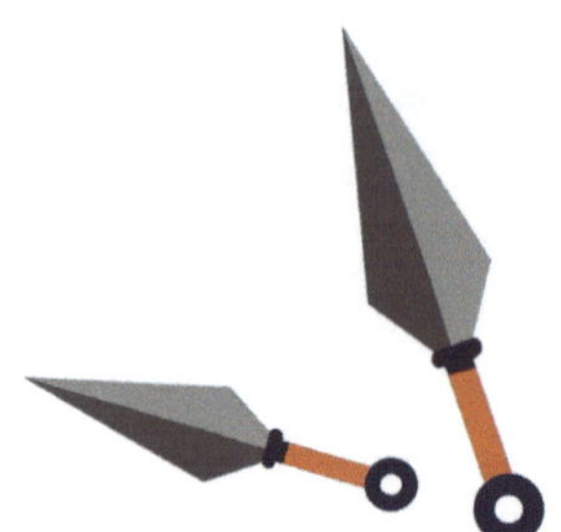

So fast no one could catch me.

Now doesn't that sound fun?

HA HA HA

If I was a ninja,

I'd study martial arts.

I'd learn such things as throwing,

Ninja stars and darts.

Today I'll be a ninja.

But when tomorrow's here,

My Imagination

Will try a new career.

Other titles by
Krystal Whitehead:

I Wish I Was A Pirate

COMING SOON

I Wish I Was A Princess

I Wish I Was A Cowboy

I Wish I Was A Cowgirl